This book belongs to:

_____

Quiet Bunny
& Noisy Puppy

STERLING CHILDREN'S BOOKS
New York
An Imprint of Sterling Publishing
387 Park Avenue South
New York, NY 10016

To Maureen, who is as cute as a bunny and as playful as a puppy. –LM

ISBN 978-1-4027-8559-7

Library of Congress Cataloging-in-Publication Data
McCue, Lisa.
  Quiet Bunny & Noisy Puppy / by Lisa McCue.
    p. cm.
  Summary: Quiet Bunny's forest friends all hibernate or go south for the winter, but when he meets a puppy from a
nearby farm the two become the best of friends, even though they are opposites in every way.
  ISBN 978-1-4027-8559-7
  [1. Rabbits--Fiction. 2. Dogs--Fiction. 3. Friendship--Fiction. 4. Winter--Fiction.] I. Title. II. Title: Quiet Bunny and
Noisy Puppy.
  PZ7.M4784149Quic 2011
  [E]--dc22
                                                                                                2010046776

Distributed in Canada by Sterling Publishing
c/o Canadian Manda Group, 165 Dufferin Street
Toronto, Ontario, Canada M6K 3H6
Distributed in the United Kingdom by GMC Distribution Services
Castle Place, 166 High Street, Lewes, East Sussex, England BN7 1XU
Distributed in Australia by Capricorn Link (Australia) Pty. Ltd.
P.O. Box 704, Windsor, NSW 2756, Australia

For information about custom editions, special sales, and premium and corporate purchases, please contact
Sterling Special Sales at 800-805-5489 or specialsales@sterlingpublishing.com.

Manufactured in China
Lot #:
2 4 6 8 10 9 7 5 3 1
06/11

www.sterlingpublishing.com/kids

Quiet Bunny
& Noisy Puppy

Lisa McCue

STERLING CHILDREN'S BOOKS
New York

Quiet Bunny woke up one morning to find the forest blanketed in snow.
Big white snowflakes swirled around his head as he hopped through the forest.

I wish I had someone to play with in the snow, thought Quiet Bunny.
He hopped to Bear Cub's den.

Thump, Thump, Thump

Mother Bear peeked out. "I'm sorry, Quiet Bunny.
Bear Cub cannot play," she said with a big yawn.
"We are getting ready to hibernate. See you in the spring."

Quiet Bunny hopped to the pond.
But the ducks had flown south for the winter,
and Bullfrog was fast asleep under the ice.
Quiet Bunny had no one to play with.

Arf arf arf rrruff grrrrrr rrruff arf

Suddenly, out from behind a snowdrift leaped a puppy.

The puppy jumped up and down.

Quiet Bunny sat very still.

"Hello," yipped the puppy, "I live on the farm. Want to play?"

Quiet Bunny had never met a puppy before.
And the puppy was not at all like Quiet Bunny.
Quiet Bunny had large floppy ears.
The puppy's ears were small and pointy.

Quiet Bunny had a short fluffy tail.
The puppy's tail was long and skinny.
Quiet Bunny was quiet.
The puppy was NOISY!

Arf arf arf rrrrruff woof woof rrrrruff

Owl heard Noisy Puppy's loud barking.

From her snowy perch high above in the tree she fluttered down.

"Quiet Bunny," she hooted, "farm animals and forest animals

may be different, but we are all animals.

You can be different and still be friends."

Quiet Bunny and Noisy Puppy watched Owl fly away.

They looked at each other, then . . .

. . . they began to play!
Quiet Bunny jumped over the snowy tree branches.
Noisy Puppy wriggled under them.

Arfrrruff

Quiet Bunny scampered around the frozen pond.
Noisy Puppy slid across it.

They played hide and seek.
Quiet Bunny hid inside a log.
Noisy Puppy searched outside it.

They played tag.

Quiet Bunny hopped up the hill.

Noisy Puppy tumbled down.

Rrruff woof arf arf arf

Quiet Bunny and Noisy Puppy were opposite in every way,
but soon became best friends.

Every morning Noisy Puppy left the farm to play with Quiet Bunny in the forest, and the winter days passed happily by.

Then the snow began to melt, and the crocuses bloomed.
As the friends frolicked about the meadow, Quiet Bunny noticed
a flock of birds returning to the forest. Spring was coming!

Quiet Bunny happily jumped up and down.

Noisy Puppy sat silent.

"Now that it is spring, I cannot play in the forest every day,"
said Noisy Puppy sadly. "It is time for me to work on the farm."

Quiet Bunny stayed on the hillside and watched as Noisy Puppy headed home.

Rrruff arf arf rrruff woof woof rrruff arf arf arf ...

The next morning Bear Cub woke up, ready to play. Bullfrog hopped about, and the ducks splashed down in the pond. Quiet Bunny was happy to see his forest friends. But he missed Noisy Puppy.

Spring turned to summer, and summer to fall.

Quiet Bunny woke up one morning to find
the forest blanketed in snow. He heard a sound.

Arf arf arf rrruff grrrrrrr
Rrruff arf woof

The friends looked more different than ever.
Noisy Puppy had grown bigger.
Quiet Bunny had stayed little.
But inside they were the same.

The two best friends romped through the forest—over, under, around, across, in, out, up, and down.

Rrrrufff woof arf arf arf... woof